BEASTS OF OLYMPUS

BEAST KEEPER

Lucy Coats is the author of more than thirty books for readers of all ages, including *Atticus the Storyteller's 100 Greek Myths*, which was shortlisted for the Blue Peter Book Award. She began her storytelling career as a bookseller, editor and journalist, and has been fascinated by myths and legends ever since she can remember. She lives in deepest south Northamptonshire with her husband and three unruly dogs. When she is not writing, she cooks, grows vegetables and sits in her stone circle, looking at the stars.

BEASTS OF OLYMPUS

BEAST KEEPER

LUCY COATS

with illustrations by
David Roberts

Piccadilly
PRESS

First published in Great Britain in 2015
by Piccadilly Press
Northburgh House, 10 Northburgh Street, London EC1V 0AT
www.piccadillypress.co.uk

Text copyright © Lucy Coats, 2015
Illustrations copyright © David Roberts, 2015

A CIP catalogue record for this book is available
from the British Library.

ISBN: 978–1–8481–2439–4

1 3 5 7 9 10 8 6 4 2

Typeset in Bembo by Palimpsest Book Production Limited,
Falkirk, Stirlingshire

Printed in the UK by Clays Ltd, St Ives plc

Piccadilly Press is an imprint of the Bonnier Publishing Group
www.bonnierpublishing.com

For Findlay, Lochlan and Paloma from
their Grande-Tante Ancienne

1

THE GOD FATHER

Demon was chatting to the chickens about eggs when his dad arrived. He'd never met his dad before, but he knew it was him all right. His dad had:

Thick, hairy goaty legs.

Big curly horns.

Yellow eyes with black slitty pupils.

No clothes to speak of.

And a set of silver reed pipes.

Demon's dad was a god.

'*Foxgodfoxgodfoxgod-runrunrun!*' The chickens scattered across the yard, gabbling and squawking in terror. Demon knelt in the dirt and bowed his head. He wasn't too sure if that's what you did with a dad, but it was certainly what you did with a god. Especially if that god was Pan, ruler of forests and all wild creatures. A god who could call up a pack of ravening bears that would rip you to bits in an instant.

'Pandemonius, my boy!' said his dad. Pan's voice was like mossy bark on ancient trees. It was deep and velvety with a hint of crumbly roughness at the edges.

Even though it was Demon's real name, no one had ever called him Pandemonius. Even the mountain wolves called him Demon — and they tended to be rather formal in their speech. Demon was about to tell his dad how silly his full name sounded when he felt a pair of huge hands under his armpits. He was lifted up into a godhug that smelled of pungent green things, goaty musk and old, stale blood.

'Good to meet you at last, my son. C'mon, let's

find your dear mother, Carys, and get your things together. Haven't seen her in far too long. Not since you arrived in the world, in fact. By Zeus's beard, how time flies.'

About two minutes later, a confused Demon found himself in a corner of the hut he shared with his mother. As he packed his few possessions into a bundle he could see his dad whispering in his mum's ear. When she'd seen Demon and his father walk in together she'd dropped her best herb-chopping knife on the hard dirt floor. It had nearly cut off her big toe. Now she kept saying, '*But . . . but . . . but . . .*' in a high-pitched voice. She sounded like Demon's little black lamb Barley did when he wanted milk. She might as well have kept quiet. Pan stomped over her *buts* like a charging centaur.

'Pandemonius is coming with me,' he said at last. 'And that's final. You don't want to offend the gods by refusing to let him go, do you?'

There was nothing much Demon's mum could say to that, really. Mortals who offended gods usually ended up as little piles of scorched ash, or as trees or rocks. In the end, Pan dragged Demon forcibly out of the door with nothing more than a quick goodbye kiss and hug from his mum. A weeping Carys was left behind, waving a damp hankie.

Demon felt like crying too. His mum was his whole family. He felt a fat bumpy lump swelling bigger and bigger in his throat until he nearly couldn't breathe. He didn't dare ask where he was being taken, or what for. Even if he had dared, he didn't know what to call his father anyway. Your Godness? Your Holiness? Your Dadness? Until a few minutes ago he'd been an ordinary eleven-year-old boy, living with his mum near an ordinary village in the middle of Arcadia. He spent his days looking after the goats and sheep and chickens, and hoeing the vegetables.

Admittedly, the fact that he could talk to animals *was* out of the ordinary. But everyone around his home knew he was the child of a god, and things like that happened to half-god kids. No one took much notice, really, except for the local farmers calling him in when their beasts were sick. Demon could ask the animals what was wrong and his mum could say what herbs to prescribe for them. All the farmers got used to hearing Demon tell them that a sheep was saying, 'my belly hurts' instead of just 'baaaaah'. Now he was being wrenched away suddenly from everything he knew by a father he didn't even know how to talk to.

When they got to the edge of the forest, Pan stopped.

'IRIS!' the god bellowed. 'EXPRESS FOR TWO! OLYMPUS-BOUND!'

Demon felt his fat bumpy throat lump get bigger still. Olympus? Why was he being taken up to Mount Olympus? Wasn't that the huge mountain where all the gods lived in shiny palaces in the sky? What were they going to do to him? A horrid thought hit his brain like a speeding arrow. He couldn't remember if the gods still liked human sacrifices or not. Perhaps that was what he was wanted for! Only . . . why had he packed all his stuff if they were just going to kill him? It wasn't like Zeus was going to want his spare cloak, was it? Just then, right in front of his eyes, a rainbow burst from the sky and landed at their feet.

'Hop on, son,' said Pan. 'Hold tight to me. The Iris Express can seem a bit fast if you're not used to it.'

Demon did as he was told. He squeezed his eyes shut and hung on to Pan's big hairy waist. He felt his stomach drop away behind him. There was a loud whooshing sound and a strong smell of flowers. *Wild roses*, he thought, sniffing cautiously. He opened one eye a crack and looked down. Then he wished he hadn't. He was standing on a see-through wisp of rainbow that was whizzing up and arching into the sky. The earth was getting smaller and smaller behind him. The whole of Greece was laid out below like a wiggly green and amber hand in a dark purple pool of sea. He was just about to scream with terror when there was another whoosh and a thump. They burst through a misty barrier and landed. Demon felt the shock of it vibrate right through the soles of his feet. He lost his grip on his dad and fell, *bump!* on his bottom.

'Here we are,' said Pan, picking Demon up and dusting him off. He strode down off the rainbow towards some shining white temples.

Everything was enormous and looked very clean on Olympus (though Demon could smell an odd and rather nasty sort of pooey stench in the air). There were all kinds of nymphs and cherubs flitting about everywhere among gigantic multicoloured blooms and trees that had bunches of silvery golden fruit hanging from them. Demon had to run to keep up with Pan. His bundle of clothes banged against his back. Suddenly he felt really angry. How dare his dad just turn up and kidnap him like this without telling him anything? It wasn't *fair*! If he was going to be sizzled and frizzled as a sacrifice he wanted to know why. In his fury, he totally forgot about being frightened of the gods. Before he could stop himself, Demon began to shout at his dad's back.

'Hey!' he yelled. 'Hey, you! Stop!'

Pan stopped. He turned round very slowly, his eyes flashing green fire. The nymphs and cherubs flicked out of sight rather abruptly.

'Are you yelling *"Hey, you!"* at ME, boy?' he asked, very quietly.

Demon gulped a bit, but he wasn't going to back down. He nodded. His mum always said his worst fault was that he never knew when to be polite and keep his mouth shut in front of his elders and betters, but this time he just didn't care. His dad had ignored him for his whole life, then ripped him away from everything and everyone he knew and loved. Pan hadn't even said please. It wasn't right, and Demon was going to find out why he was here if it killed him. Which it probably would in about three seconds' time.

'Yes. Um, Sir-Your Godness-Pan-Dad. I w-want to k-know w-what you're g-going to d-do to me.' Demon didn't want his voice to stammer and stumble, but it seemed to have a mind of its own. He cleared his throat and tried again. 'If I'm going to be a sacrifice to the gods, I think you should have let me say goodbye to Mum properly first. She's going to be really upset with you when I'm dead.'

Pan looked at him. The green fire in his eyes

died and his mouth opened in a great windy gust of laughter that nearly knocked Demon backwards.

'Sacrifice to the gods? Is that what you thought you were here for? My own son? Did you hear that, nymphs, a SACRIFICE! That's a good one!' He laughed some more, and the nymphs and cherubs flicked into view again, looking relieved. Pan scratched at a curly horn and ran a hand through his wild hair. Bits of bark, twigs and dead leaves fell out in showers. 'By Zeus's toenails! I told your dear mother, but I forgot I hadn't told you. C'mon, boy, follow me, quick as you like. I think it's high time I took you to see the Stables of the Gods.'

2

THE STABLES OF THE GODS

The Stables of the Gods were extremely smelly. There was no getting around it. As they got nearer to the long tall building a stink like a mixture of centuries-old dead fish and a thousand years of ancient poo filled Demon's nostrils. There was a roaring rumpus of beasts and monsters in every pen and stable. The noise was indescribably loud. Pan backed out of the stable and put his hands over his hairy ears. He beckoned Demon over to a bench under a tree a little way away, where it was a bit quieter. He still had to shout, though.

'All the gods and goddesses are complaining about the stink getting into their clothes – and the racket is spoiling everyone's sleep. Old Silenus the satyr looked after the beasts for ages, but then he annoyed Hera one time too many. So she got Zeus to banish him down to earth. A place called Lydia, I think, near some king's palace. Dionysus got him out of trouble there too . . . Anyway, then I had one of my fauns look after the stables, but he got bitten by a Basilisk. Since then it's all gone to Hades a bit.' He cleared his throat. 'Zeus asked me to find someone who was good with animals. I thought you might like to have a go at the job. You've done pretty well with mortal beasts, and immortal creatures aren't so very different – barring a fang or two.'

Demon opened his mouth then shut it again. He didn't know what to say. But he felt quite relieved that he wasn't going to be a sacrifice.

Pan went on, 'Zeus and the others are prepared to give you a trial run as a stable boy to see if you're any good at it – and we'll set you up with a magical healing thingummyjig so you don't get killed in the first five minutes. If you're a success, you'll get an official title and some proper pay. What do you say, boy? Will you give it a go?'

Demon looked at his dad. There was bound to be a catch — there always was with gods, his mum had drummed that into him since he was tiny.

'Do I get a choice?' he asked.

Pan looked at him and smiled widely. His teeth were square and yellow and flecked with green and red. 'I know how much you love animals, Pandemonius, and how they love you back. Of course you have a choice,' he paused here and smiled a little wider — it was a dangerous smile this time. 'But on the other hand, if you offend all the Olympians by refusing even to have a try . . .'

Pan didn't have to say any more than that. Demon knew he was stuck with the job for now, whether he wanted it or not. And it was true what his dad had said — he did love animals. Perhaps it would be OK. It might even be exciting. 'What do I have to do?' he asked.

'Hephaestus will fill you in,' said Pan. 'He's the

smith god, you know. Good at metalwork and so on. Clever fellow with his hands. He makes all sorts of marvellous thingies for us at his forge. I'll take you to meet him now. Maybe if you ask nicely he'll lend you one of his metal men to help with the clean-up.' He sniffed, his large nostrils flaring like a hound on a scent. 'Don't take too long to get rid of the pong or the goddesses are bound to come after you. Best not to tempt them.'

On this comforting thought Pan turned and walked away. Demon followed him, trying hard not to think of angry goddesses and piles of charcoal.

Hephaestus turned out to live inside a mountain. He was hammering at his forge when Pan and Demon walked in.

'Just a minute,' he yelled. 'Got to finish this sword for Ares. He's always breaking them in one of his idiotic wars, the crazy fool.'

Demon watched with amazement. Hephaestus grabbed the blazing metal with his bare hands, and a man-like creature that seemed to be made of gold and silver pumped the bellows.

'One of my automaton robots,' shouted Hephaestus when he saw Demon looking at the metal creature. 'I made it a while ago to help in the forge. Not much for chatting, but great at keeping the heat steady. I've got lots of different kinds. Useful creatures, these robots.'

There was a final clang and then the smith god put down his tools.

'Ah,' he continued. 'Young Pandemonius, is it? We've all heard about you and the wonders you're going to perform in the stables. Your dad's been singing your praises, you know. Very proud of you. Chip off the old block, eh?'

Pan cleared his throat and looked embarrassed (if a god could look embarrassed).

'I've got to go now,' Demon's father said hurriedly, his slitted yellow eyes darting from side to side. 'There's trouble with my satyrs in Caria — always fighting, those boys. Look after my son, Heffy. Don't want him eaten! Now, Pandemonius, you do what Hephaestus tells you. He'll sort you out. Give you what you need to get started, that sort of thing. I'll come and see you again when I can.'

Pan fumbled in what seemed to be a pocket in his hairy thigh, pulled out a battered set of reed pipes and handed them to Demon. 'My spare set. Good for calming awkward beasts. Just tootle away and they should settle down. Be careful, though,' he said. 'It doesn't always work on all of them, so you take care.' He patted Demon on the head, nearly knocking him over, and turned away.

Demon felt the bumpy throat lump come back as the forest god left. He hadn't known his dad was proud of him, or that Pan had been watching over him and it made him go a bit warm and fuzzy inside. Maybe he might get to know his dad properly now – Pan had said he'd come back, after all. Demon just hoped he wasn't going to mess his new job up though. Immortal beasts were sure to be very different to chickens and goats, whatever Pan thought.

'Now,' said Hephaestus in a voice that was meant to be reassuring, but somehow wasn't, 'sit on this barrel here and have a cup of ambrosia. Then we'll go and get you settled in.' He handed Demon a goblet full of golden liquid that smelled wonderful. Unfortunately it didn't taste quite as good as it smelled and Demon spat it out at once.

'Ugh!' he said, spluttering. 'What's *that*? It's really disgusting.'

'That's the food of the gods,' said Hephaestus. 'Ambrosia, we call it – comes in both liquid and cake form. You might like the cake more. You'd better get used to it, boy, because it's all there is up here unless it's a feast day. Anyway, it's good for you. Makes you stronger than normal mortals. Gives you muscles like a hero. Ah, that reminds me. Better give you one of my healing charms or your puny mortal body won't last any time at all in the stables.'

He walked over to a shelf and took down a thin bronze collar shaped like two curled snakes biting their own tails. The snakes had ruby eyes and seemed to writhe as Demon looked at them.

'Put this round your neck. The snakes are called Offy and Yukus. They'll sort out pretty much anything in the way of bites or stings or anything else those vicious creatures might throw at you. Just try not to get your head chomped off. That'll be almost impossible for them to mend. Now, let's go to the stables and introduce you to the beasts properly.'

3

THE BEASTLY BEASTS

As Demon curled up in a pile of straw that night, he knew he had never been more exhausted. When they got to the stables, Hephaestus had pointed out which creature was which and shown him where the brooms and buckets and pitchforks and barrows were. He explained how to get to the muckheap and how to use the magic chute that sent all the poo down to feed the hundred-armed monsters in Tartarus.

'Mind you don't fall down there yourself,

young Pandemonius,' the smith god told him. 'Tartarus is where Zeus sends all the real baddies to be punished by his brother Hades. It's full of fiery pits and things you don't even want to think about.' With that cheerful thought, Hephaestus patted him on the head.

'There's a loft up above the unicorns. You can sleep there. I think the faun left his blanket. The nymphs come round with fresh ambrosia cakes for you and leftovers for the beasts twice a day – and you can get water from the spring outside. Remember to thank Melanie the water naiad, though, or she'll cover you in waterweed. If you have any problems come and find me.' Then he waved casually and walked out, leaving Demon all alone in the midst of the noise and chaos – and the smell.

Demon put his bundle down and just stood there. 'Talk about being thrown in at the deep end,' he muttered resentfully. There was just so much to take in. He'd never seen so many different beasts – most of them dangerous, magical and with hard-to-remember names. He needed to think.

'SHUT UP!' he bawled.

To his surprise, it worked. Kind of. The noise fell by at least a quarter.

'Thank you. Now let's sort this mess out. Who's the smelliest? I'm going to start with them.'

Immediately the noise rose to a higher pitch than before. But Demon could hear two words being repeated over and over in lots of strange and different voices.

'STINKY COWS!

STINKY COWS!

STINKY COWS!'

He looked down the stables and saw a huge pen with some rather shamefaced horned heads hanging over the rails. The horns were golden, and had stars on the ends, which shone with a gentle light. They belonged to some rather fat cows, with coats the colour of a red sunset. Demon knew they must be the famous Cattle of the Sun, resting after months of being dragged back from the lands of Geryon the Giant by the hero Heracles.

'We can't help it,' the cows all mooed. 'It's that leftover ambrosia cake. It doesn't suit our stomachs. It gives us terrible gas!'

The other beasts jeered and hissed as Demon walked down towards them, avoiding a row of snapping jaws and tearing claws on either side.

'STINKY COWS!

STINKY COWS!

STINKY COWS!'

It was sadly true. The Cattle of the Sun stank more than any of the other beasts. They reeked. They honked. No wonder the whole of Olympus smelled of poo. The stink was so strong that Demon staggered back from their pen and bumped into the barred door of a stable opposite. A large clawed paw whipped out and caught him on the shoulder, ripping his tunic and tearing deep into his flesh. Demon jerked away and fell to his knees, trying not to scream. Immediately the snakes on his collar whipped round and plunged their tongues into the wound. Miraculously, it stopped hurting at once, and he could feel the gash closing up.

'Th-th-thanks,' he whispered, feeling the now-smooth skin with trembling fingers. Offy and Yukus coiled themselves back around his neck.

'It wasssss our pleasssssure,' they hissed into his ear.

Demon got up slowly and turned round. A huge creature with the head and wings of an eagle and a lion's body stared at him with its golden eyes. It was as tall as a donkey, with a rough, tawny coat, and a sharp curved beak that looked as if it could crack rocks. Demon walked forward and put his hands on the bars. It was important he didn't look afraid. Animals didn't respect you if you were frightened.

'You're a griffin, aren't you?' he asked. The

creature spat, and the spit sizzled slightly as it hit the ground.

'Yes,' it said aggressively. 'So?' Its scary beak darted out and clacked shut just by Demon's ear. He dodged away just in time to avoid another serious injury.

'*So* I'm here to look after you all,' Demon said in a loud, firm voice (even though he was quaking like a pile of jellied eels inside). 'Zeus's orders. If you want clean beds and someone to listen to what you need, then you'll leave off the clawing and biting stuff.' His voice dropped, and became what he hoped was threatening. 'I'm quite sure Zeus would be VERY interested to hear that you were trying to kill the stable boy HE appointed. He wouldn't be very pleased. In fact he might even come and PAY YOU A VISIT.' Demon held his breath and waited. Surely no one wanted a visit from Zeus?

But the griffin wasn't backing down. It spat at him again, hitting the hem of his chiton and making a big smoking hole in it. 'Hate humans,' it hissed aggressively.

Demon crouched down in front of it. 'Why do you hate humans?' he asked.

The griffin snorted. 'We ALL hate humans,' it snarled. ''Specially half-god humans like you. That's what most of the heroes are, see. The gods send us down to the earthly realms to fight them or give them some sort of adventure. We're immortal, of course, so we can't really die. After we get "killed" down there we come back up here to recover. And then they send us back down to do it all over again. No one really cares about us beasts. We're just entertainment – a bit of fun for the gods – their dangerous little pets.'

Then a whole chorus of angry voices joined in.

Yes. A bit of fun.

You should see my spear scars.

That Heracles is the worst. Always off destroying us beasts.

I got a lump of burning lead shoved down my throat!

I got my tails chopped off!

I have to spend every day tearing out some poor bloke's liver – and I don't even like liver!

IT'S NOT FAIR!

As the noise grew louder and louder, Demon remembered his dad's pipes. He got them out and blew a long series of silvery notes. It was like a miracle. Immediate silence.

'You poor things,' he said into the quiet. 'That sounds terrible. But look at me! I'm not a hero. I may be the son of Pan, but really I'm just a scrawny boy who loves all creatures, tame or wild. And I'd never hurt any of you.' He paused. 'I-I'm all alone up here s-so I'd really like us to be friends. I promise to do my best for you. Will you help me?'

One of the tears Demon had been holding back for so long escaped and trickled down his cheek. He brushed it away crossly as the griffin glared down its beak at him, poked out a very long forked tongue and licked its beak meaningfully.

'You threatened us with a visit from Zeus, scrawny Pan's kid. I don't like threats. How about the rest of you?'

Any normal human would just have heard a cacophony of growls and moos and squeaks and snarls and roars and barks and howls.

Demon heard:

NO!

4
THE STABLE BOY

Demon was exhausted every single night from then on. He just curled up in his bed of straw, pulled the faun's spider-silk blanket over him, and slept like a dead person. He was bitten and bruised and clawed and stung at least twenty times a day by various beasts. Offy and Yukus had to work on him pretty much full time to keep him alive. Hephaestus had lent him one of his metal robots for a few days, and together they had shovelled and forked and barrowed what seemed like enough beast poo to create several new muckheap mountains. Demon thought he could hear the hundred-armed monsters roaring their appreciation for their massive poo feast from the bottom of the chute.

Demon had talked to Hephaestus about the Cattle of the Sun and their windy stomachs. Thankfully the smith god had asked Helios the sun god to send up some of the special golden hay he fed his horses at the same time as he delivered the silver straw the beasts slept on That had solved the problem, and now the Stables sparkled and shone and – more to the point – smelled of nothing more than the aroma of clean, well-fed beasts. There was no chance of the gods or goddesses complaining now, he hoped.

He didn't have much to do with the gods really, apart from Hephaestus, who was turning out to be quite kind for an Immortal. There was just the occasional flash, whoosh and thump as the Iris Express landed, or a brief message via a cherub requesting that this beast or that be made ready to go down to the earthly realms, or the crack and roar of thunder and lightning from Zeus and Hera's big palace on the farthest hill. Demon didn't mind – the less he had to do with the gods the better, he thought. He was a bit surprised his dad hadn't been back to see him, though. Maybe it was because Pan didn't actually live up on Olympus. He was happier in the green forests of Arcadia, back down on earth. Demon tried hard not to feel resentful about that. He missed the forests too, and all his animal friends like the wolves and the rabbits – and the lambs and chickens too, of course.

Outside his work at the stables, Demon was almost happy. He thought about his mum a lot, of course, but the nymphs and naiads and dryads soon began to treat him like a little brother. They teased him and told him snippets of gossip about the gods and goddesses. In this way he learned that Zeus was a terrible flirt who was always getting into trouble with Hera, that Dionysus had invented a new kind of grape drink which made everybody very giggly and silly, that Aphrodite had just redecorated her palace in fifty different shades of pink and was always meddling in the lives of mortal lovers . . . and that Hera was best avoided at all times if you knew what was good for you.

Inside the stables he was learning to deal with his charges little by little. The beasts saw that he really did seem to care about their welfare, and most of them tolerated him. Even the griffin was becoming friendlier. It only bit him half-heartedly now, and Demon suspected it might even have a sense of humour when he found out that it liked to hide in a dark corner of its cage and then leap out at him. It was certainly becoming much chattier and it seemed to enjoy giving him advice. It had even told him its name – Arnie. Demon had had to bite the inside of his cheek hard to stop himself sniggering at that. Arnie just didn't seem a very dignified name for such an enormous creature.

The job he liked best was exercising the little Ethiopian winged horses. He brushed and brushed them until their coats shone like ivory and onyx and bronze, and then he polished their little gold horns and wiped their wings down with scented oil he'd found in the stores. The boss horse was called Keith, and at first he had tended to snap and bite and rear when Demon tried to get on his back. However, after Demon had discovered that Keith liked his left ear scratched in a certain way, they'd come to an arrangement. Ten minutes scratching equalled a half-hour exercise flight. Demon thought that was *very* fair. So every day he found himself soaring through the air over Olympus at the head of a pack of six flying horses. They looped the loop over Hephaestus's mountain and chased the fiery spark spirits high into the atmosphere. It was definitely better than herding goats and sheep on the farm, he reckoned.

Not all the beasts were as easy to please as Keith, though. It had taken him a whole week to learn how to get near enough to feed the unicorns, let alone milk them. There'd been a series of increasingly angry messages from Aphrodite (who wanted her annual unicorn milk bath), and so he'd had to get some advice.

'How do you milk a unicorn, please?' he asked Melanie the water naiad politely, as he filled the buckets at her spring. But she was busy admiring her new necklace of raindrops and wouldn't answer him. The cherubs just giggled and pelted him with petals. The nymphs were more helpful.

'They like girls,' said the head nymph, whose name was Althea.

Demon looked at her. 'Don't know if you'd noticed,' he said, slightly sarcastically, 'but I'm not a girl.'

That started a lot of giggling and nudging from the other nymphs, but Althea just gave her sisters a look and they fell silent.

'We owe you,' she said. 'Those smelly stables were just about killing our noses – we all felt really sick until you came along and cleaned up. So one of us will do it for you every morning and evening if you'll let us have the wool from the Golden Ram when you shear him. It makes the finest embroidery thread, you know, and we like it for decorating our dresses.'

'It's a deal,' said Demon. He had never sheared a winged sheep before, but he was willing to try anything to get Aphrodite off his back.

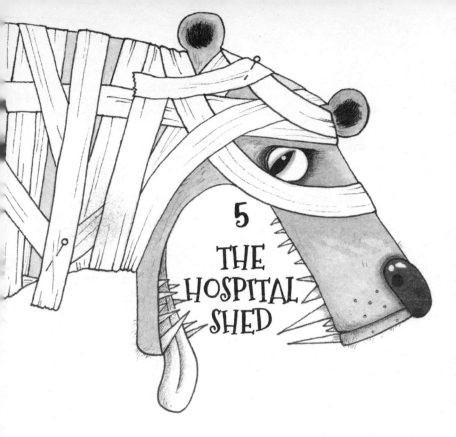

5
THE
HOSPITAL
SHED

Demon was just beginning to feel that he'd really settled into his new job when the casualties started to arrive. The Nemean Lion was the first. One morning the Iris Express landed as usual and immediately an alarm in the stables began to sound.

'Incoming wounded, incoming wounded,' squawked a carved head on the back wall. Demon had wondered what it was for, and now he knew. He started to panic at once.

'What do I do?' he asked Arnie, whose clawed toenails he was picking out at the time. It nodded towards a long, low wagon that stood propped against the end wall of the stables.

'Off you go with that,' the griffin said. 'Iris usually dumps the wounded at the foot of the Express for someone to collect and bring back here. Whoever it is needs to go in the hospital shed to be patched up. You do know where that is, don't you?'

Demon shook his head. How could he have been so stupid? On his very first day the beasts had told him they often got hurt. Why hadn't he checked out the hospital?

Demon shot out of Arnie's stable, forgetting to latch the door behind him, grabbed the stretcher wagon and started to run, cursing himself all the way. He'd treated plenty of normal animals with his mum's help, but he didn't have her healing herbs or bandages or anything here – and he absolutely hated seeing an animal in pain.

What he found at the foot of the Iris Express was worse than he could ever have imagined. A huge bald pink lion lay there, moaning in agony.

'My skin, my special skin,' it groaned.

Demon approached cautiously. Its skin might have gone, but its claws and teeth were definitely still present.

'I'm Demon,' he said softly, squatting down beside it. 'Will you let me help you?'

The lion rolled its eyes and groaned some more as Demon hauled it onto the stretcher as gently as he could. It was really hard, and Demon was thankful for the extra muscles the ambrosia had given him. Maybe it was worth drinking the disgusting stuff after all.

By the time it was on the stretcher, the lion had bit him twice and scratched him seventeen times, but the magic snakes whipped into action and the blood stopped oozing in almost no time at all. Demon hardly noticed – he was too busy trying to work out what he should do with the poor thing.

'Over here,' yelled Arnie. The griffin flicked the door open with a paw and escaped from its open cage. 'Lucky for you I'm not the Minotaur, or you'd have been in big trouble, Pan's scrawny kid,' it said.

Arnie pointed to a big thatched shed right at the back of the stables. Demon had thought it was a storage shed of some kind but he hadn't checked it out yet. Sorting out the main stable block had taken all his time and energy. He wheeled the stretcher wagon towards the hospital shed.

When Arnie saw the Nemean Lion it whistled through its beak. 'By Chiron's hooves, mate. Who got *you*? That's a terrible state you're in.'

'Heracles,' moaned the lion. 'Hera's set him twelve impossible tasks as a punishment for killing his poor wife and children. Apparently she's got a little list marked "Labours for Heracles" and she's going to tick them off one by one.' The lion moaned some more. 'He's gone and ripped off my poor skin and made it into invincible armour. Heracles was bad enough before, but now none of us beasts are safe. I'm only the first casualty you'll have to deal with, you mark my words.'

With that, the lion's eyes rolled up in its skinless head and it fainted.

Demon looked around the shelves. There were dirty, unrolled bandages, half-empty bottles, spilled herbs and a variety of blunt instruments that looked as if they'd been used as cutlery.

'Silenus wasn't great at doctoring,' said Arnie, stating the obvious. Demon stared at the lion in despair. He hadn't a clue where to start with helping it.

Arnie came over and headbutted him gently. 'I'd have a word with Hephaestus,' it advised him. 'He's a god who cares enough to fix most things. Unlike most of the others,' it muttered angrily.

Demon sent a brief, bitter thought in Pan's direction. He'd really believed his father when he said he was going to come back. Pan could probably heal bald lions in his sleep if he wanted to – but he couldn't even be bothered to visit. At least the smith god kept his promises.

'I wish Heffy was my dad,' he grumbled, as he started to run. By the time Demon reached Hephaestus's mountain, he was panting like a boy who'd finished four marathons. He had to drink a whole glass of the revolting ambrosia before he could even speak. When he'd explained the problem, Hephaestus scratched his head.

'You need some of my magic bandages, I should think,' he said. 'I keep them around in case any of the nymphs come in here and get burned – happens sometimes when the forge is at full whack and I don't notice them standing there. The bandages should help soothe the lion – and then we can think about making him a new pelt. You can get the Caucasian Eagle to nip over to Pandora's house, on his way back from tearing old Prometheus's liver out, and ask Epimetheus if he has any skin left over from making all those furry earth animals.'

Hephaestus rummaged around on the shelves to the left of the furnace and pulled out a square green package with the familiar scent of lavender and aloe – and something Demon didn't recognise thrown in too. 'Here you are – slap those all over him for now. I'll be along in a bit to see how you're getting on.'

The Nemean Lion did look funny covered in sticky green gauze, but he also seemed to be more comfortable. Demon fed him leftover ambrosia through a straw when he woke and then the lion told him about the fight with Heracles. By the time he'd finished, Demon reckoned that if he ever met Heracles, he was going to punch the wretched hero on the nose . . . however strong and big he was. Nice people did NOT go around pulling skins off poor innocent lions – no matter what kind of task they'd been set by the Queen of the Heavens.

Later that night, Hephaestus turned up as promised. He limped into the hospital shed carrying a large silver box with brass handles, which he set down on the floor.

'Should have given you this before, really,' he said. 'It's got the same sort of magic in it as Offy and Yukus use on you – only it's for beasts. Just open it when you've got a medical emergency and in most cases you'll find it tells you what you need. Think it'll provide a cure for just about anything that happens to your beasts. There's this too.' He handed over a short length of silver rope. 'Ties anything. Expands as needed. Won't come undone. And I ground some of my calming crystals into the core of it in case your dad's pipes aren't handy. You can belt it round your chiton so it's always with you.'

Demon forgot Hephaestus was one of the gods and jumped up and hugged him. This was what a real father should be like.

'Thanks, Heffy,' he said. 'You're the best!'

Hephaestus grinned down at him and ruffled his hair.

'Irreverent cub,' he said. 'Don't you go calling Zeus "Zeusie", now, or you'll find yourself a pile of ash faster than you can blink. And mind you don't forget to send that message with the Caucasian Eagle. You definitely need new skin for the lion – but unfortunately the box won't provide enough of it. It only does patches.'

When the Caucasian Eagle returned the next day, it was carrying a small bag in its claws. 'Here you are,' it said, dropping it at Demon's feet. 'Epimetheus says that's the very last of the skin, so don't go asking for any more. Now, where's my ambrosia? Filthy stuff, but it takes away the taste of liver. I REALLY hate that wretched liver,' it grumbled, flying off to its perch and tucking its head under its wing.

Demon thanked the eagle and picked up the bag, yawning. He'd been up with the Nemean Lion all night, playing Pan's pipes to soothe it and changing its dressings in between scrubbing and tidying up the hospital shed.

'Let's have a look,' he said, upending the bag on the now shiny clean counter. There was a tiny but distinct silence as he and the lion looked at what had fallen out.

There was no getting away from it. The skin that Epimetheus had sent was spotty with a hint of fluff. It was also a strange shade of bright green.

'Er, perhaps it's just gone a bit mouldy and the colour will wash off,' Demon said in an optimistic tone.

He wasn't hopeful, though. When he brushed

at the skin, it stayed firmly green. Like new grass.

'I'll be a laughing stock,' moaned the lion. 'Lions have flat tawny skin. If you put that on me I'll be the Lesser Green-spotted Nemean Lion.'

'Think of it as a fashion statement,' said Demon encouragingly. 'I'm sure all the lady lions will love it. Would you rather stay as you are and be the Bald-coated Pink Nemean Lion?'

'Go on then,' said the lion. 'I don't care any more. I shall ask the gods to let me go into retirement in a nice lonely cave somewhere if they insist on sending me back to the earthly realms.'

The new skin fitted – just. It was a bit of a tight squeeze and there were a couple of odd bulgy lumps where Demon had had to smooth and squash bits of lion into rather too little skin – but at least the Nemean Lion looked like a lion again (though a very oddly coloured and patterned and slightly fluffy one).

Demon put him into a nice darkened stable to rest and later on Hephaestus brought over some meaty scraps from one of the gods' feasts. The lion gobbled them up in seconds. Demon's first medical emergency seemed to be over and he hadn't even needed to use the silver box. He felt quite proud of himself.

6

THE BRONZE BIRDS

All was quiet for a week or so. The Nemean Lion was getting used to its strange skin, and had recovered enough to begin some playful chasing of Artemis's five Golden-horned Deer (though it promised Demon it wouldn't hurt them). Once the rest of the beasts in the stables had seen what Demon had done for the Nemean Lion they accepted him totally – with the exception of the Giant Scorpion.

Then the carved head began to squawk again.

'Incoming wounded. Incoming wounded, lots of incoming wounded,' it shouted.

Demon rushed for the wagon. This time he remembered to lock the cage doors behind him. No one would have been happy if the Giant Scorpion had escaped. It hated everybody and liked nothing better than stabbing its huge sting into the gentler beasts and dangling them up in the air over its pincers. Demon didn't trust it an inch after he'd found out how that felt for himself, and now when he fed it he usually approached the scary creature with a long pointy fending-off stick.

When he got to the Iris Express, there was a whole flock of large, almost featherless birds scattered all over the ground. 'Heracles?' he asked. The birds nodded and clacked their beaks. What had remained of their feathers rattled as he lifted each one carefully onto his stretcher wagon.

'Careful,' said one. 'Don't cut yourself.'

When Demon looked more closely, he noticed that the feathers were made of pure, shiny bronze. He also noticed that all the birds had razor-sharp teeth inside their beaks.

'You're the Stymphalian Birds, aren't you?' he asked as he trundled them into the hospital shed. 'Do you want to tell me what happened?'

'We were just finishing off this tasty maiden we'd found washing some horrid dirty clothes in our nice clean lake – very juicy and tender she was, too – when there was this horrible noise,' squawked the bird who had spoken before. It seemed to be the leader of the flock. 'Sort of a rattly racket that got into our ears and made us fly up in the air. Next thing we knew, there were arrows coming at us from the other side of the water. We saw that horrible hero Heracles, with that huge bow of his, shooting away at us. Poor Boneyfeet over there copped an arrow right in the head – blood everywhere. Very nasty – we nearly had to leave him behind for the fishes to nibble.

'Well, we fired our bronze feathers right back at him, same as we always do – only he wouldn't stop. We were losing all our feathers so we called up to Ares when we realised we were going to be in trouble if we carried on firing – and he sent the Iris Express down for us.' The bird looked at

Demon with a bright orange eye. 'Can you fix us up? Only Ares says there's a nice island we can go to in the Black Sea. We don't like it up here on Olympus much – not enough flesh, too much ambrosia, if you know what I mean.' The bird ran a pink pointy tongue round its teeth.

'I'll give it a go,' said Demon, opening Hephaestus's magic medical box for the very first time. Soft blue symbols glowed underneath the lid.

'State the nature of your beast's emergency medical problem,' said a metallic voice.

'Um . . .' said Demon.

'Um not a recognised problem of an emergency medical nature,' said the box. 'Does not compute with data program. Please restate.'

Demon took a deep breath. He wasn't used to boxes talking to him.

'Er,' he said, stopping.

'Er not a recognised problem of an emergency medical nature,' said the box. 'Does not compute with data program. Please restate.'

'Let me do it,' said the head bird, hopping off the table and giving the box a peck. 'I'm a

Stymphalian Bird. My feathers have fallen out. I need new ones. Does that compute, you stupid square object?'

The letters under the lid glowed a sullen kind of green. 'All right, all right,' said the metallic voice sulkily. 'Just having a little joke. Feather medicine coming right up, and I hope they itch awfully while they're re-growing.' Immediately, a phial of bronze-coloured liquid popped up in the centre of the box. 'Give 'em all one drop,' said the box to Demon. 'And mind those teeth. Should be fixed in about an hour.'

Demon undid the phial and dripped a single drop into each bird's beak, careful to avoid slicing his fingers open. Sure enough, an hour later, all their bronze feathers had grown back.

'Thanks, Demon,' they said as they flew off to catch the Iris Express down to their new home in the Black Sea. 'We've left you a few old feathers on the side. They're useful for cutting stuff up. Or stabbing that Heracles if he shows his face up here.'

Demon put the feathers away carefully in a

drawer. 'If that Heracles comes anywhere near my beasts again, I *will* stab him,' he said. 'Even if he does have muscles like tree roots.'

'You're all right for a half-god human, Pan's scrawny kid,' Arnie said to him. 'At least you seem to hate that horrible Heracles as much as we do.'

Demon stroked its feathers.

'One day I'll give him what he deserves,' he said. 'No one treats my beasts like that.'

Arnie pecked him gently, only drawing a little blood this time.

'Your beasts now, are we? I wonder what Zeus will have to say about that, stable boy!'

Demon found out just how empty his brave words were when Poseidon sent yet another one of Heracles' victims up to Olympus. The Cretan Bull had been stabbed in the heart, and its fire had gone out completely. If it hadn't been immortal it would have been dead.

'HERACLES!' Demon yelled down the Iris Express as he hauled the bull onto his stretcher with his silver rope. 'I'm warning you! ONE more, just

ONE more, and I'm coming down to sort you out.'

There was no answer, but suddenly Demon felt as if a hundred gods' and goddesses' ears were listening to him. It was not a comfortable feeling at all, and Demon had the troubling thought that, once again, his big mouth might have got him into trouble. But Demon soon forgot about it in the commotion of treating his new patient.

7

THE ETERNAL FLAME

Restarting the Cretan Bull's fire took Demon nearly a week. Back and forth, back and forth he went to Hephaestus's mountain, carrying bucketload after bucketload of hot coals from the forge. The poor creature was beside itself with panic, and if he hadn't had his magic silver rope to keep it tied down, it would have gored him at least a hundred times with its golden horns. It was not a co-operative patient at all.

'C'mon, Bull,' he pleaded as he tipped yet

another scoop of hot coals carefully down its throat.

It was no good. The bull's thrashing and tossing was gradually becoming weaker and weaker. All that was coming from its normally fiery fifth stomach was a wet sloshing sound. Demon couldn't think what to do. The magic box had mended the stab wound easily enough and had told him to fetch the hot coals – but the treatment wasn't working. He opened the box once again.

'State the nature of your beast's emergency medical problem,' said the now familiar metallic voice.

'Same as before,' said Demon. 'I can't restart the Cretan Bull's fire. The coals aren't working. What else can I do?'

The box was silent for a moment, then the symbols under the lid began to flash orange and there was a series of short beeps. A thin wavering tube appeared out of the box. It had a flat silver disc on the end. The tube swayed over towards the bull, elongating as it went, and then the silver disc laid itself against the Bull's fifth stomach.

'Diagnostics in progress,' said the box. 'Please wait.' After a moment the tube whipped back into the box.

'Well?' asked Demon anxiously. 'What did you find out?' *And why do you have to use stupid long words like diagnostics?* he thought but didn't say, because by now he'd found out that the box could be a bit temperamental if he wasn't polite to it.

'Diagnostics have detected a case of bovine pentagastric marine pyrosaturitis,' said the box proudly. It sounded very smug.

Demon bit his tongue to keep himself from shouting. He needed the box's help too badly to annoy the stupid thing.

'Could you please explain what that is?' he said in his politest voice.

The box made a purring sound. 'It means you've got loads of seawater in the creature's fire-making equipment,' it said.

'Do you have a cure?' Demon asked.

There was a whirring noise as a small silver cauldron rose out of the box and floated into Demon's lap.

'Beast patient will be cured by eternal flame. Service does not provide eternal flame at present.' The box snapped shut with a very final sort of sound.

Demon stood up, holding the silver cauldron. What he felt like was kicking the magic medicine box, but curing his patient came first. Only he still didn't know how.

What do I do now? he thought as he fluffed up the silvery straw round the Cretan Bull and made it as comfortable as he could. He decided to go and ask Hephaestus. Eternal flame sounded like the smith god's kind of thing. But when he got to the forge under the mountain, Hephaestus wasn't there.

'Gone to deliver two of my brothers to some mortal queen,' said the gold and silver automaton robot who was keeping the fire going.

Demon's stomach slid down to somewhere near his feet.

'You, er, you don't have any eternal flame in here, do you?' he asked, all in a rush. Demon still wasn't used to talking to Hephaestus's metal people.

'Nope,' it said, and it turned back to the fire. Hephaestus was right – the forge robot definitely wasn't one for talking much.

Demon trudged back to the stables. Perhaps Arnie would know.

'Eternal flame?' asked Arnie. 'That's the stuff in Hestia's hearth. Why do you want to know?'

Demon explained about the Cretan Bull's waterlogged fifth stomach. Arnie just opened its beak wide and cackled. 'Good luck with that. The last one to steal some eternal flame was Prometheus – and, as you know, he's currently strapped to a mountain having his liver pecked out on a daily basis by our friend the Caucasian Eagle.'

By now, Demon's stomach had dropped past his feet and was well on its way back down to earth. He went to check on the bull to see if, by some miracle, it was better. It wasn't. He was going to have to visit a goddess he didn't know and ask her a favour.

Goddesses weren't known for doing favours for anyone – let alone a stable boy. She'd definitely want something in return. Or maybe she'd be so grateful he'd got rid of the cow-poo smell that she'd give him the flame for free, he thought hopefully. He patted the bull. Too weak to do anything else, it groaned pathetically.

'I'll be back soon,' he promised, keeping his fingers crossed. He just hoped it was true.

Althea the nymph agreed to show Demon the way to Hestia's palace. He felt very conspicuous and very small as he walked past the huge pillared front doors of the palaces. Althea was chattering away as normal, telling him who lived where, but he was too nervous to listen properly. Hestia's palace turned out to be slap-bang in the middle.

'Will you come in with me, Althea?' he asked.

The nymph just giggled and shook her head, tossing her long floaty hair.

'Nymphs are not allowed in the dwellings unless invited,' she said. 'And anyway, I've got some sunflowers to polish for Helios.'

She flitted away, leaving Demon standing in front of a door with intricate carvings of cooking pots and kitchen utensils. He raised his hand to knock, but the door creaked open before he could get his knuckles to it.

'Come in, little stable boy,' said a deep voice. It sounded like cream and honey dripping onto hot rocks.

Demon forced his feet to walk forward. He clutched his small silver cauldron tightly as he went into a vast dark room. There was a fire right in the middle of it. Over it a huge silver cauldron – an exact copy of the one he was carrying – was hanging from a hook. There was a long-handled spoon in the cauldron, stirring all by itself. On the other side of the fire stood a figure. Demon fell to his knees.

'Oh, do get up and tell me what you want, Pandemonius,' said the voice. 'I'm not going to cook you. Yet.' Hestia laughed as Demon got up, trembling. 'Only joking about the cooking,' said the goddess.

Demon didn't believe her. But he couldn't afford to think about that. He wasn't here for himself, so he cleared his throat and made himself brave for the Cretan Bull's sake.

'I'm sorry to bother you, Your Goddessness,' he asked. 'But would it be possible to have a tiny bit of your eternal flame, please? Only it's needed to cure one of the beasts in the stables.' He squeezed his eyes shut and crossed his fingers, hoping.

There was a rustle in front of him and a smell of loukoumathes, the small honey cakes that were his very favourite things to eat in the whole world. He thought of his mum mixing the batter and giving him the bowl to lick. A sudden rush of homesickness came over him. Why did he have to be up here with the stupid gods? Why couldn't he just go back to how it was before? Why couldn't his father have just left them alone?

Then Demon felt the little silver cauldron being plucked from his fingers. He cautiously opened one eye, blinked hurriedly and opened the other eye. Then he remembered that he was standing in front of a scary cooking goddess. Hestia was examining the cauldron. She was very tall and quite plump, and she was wearing an apron embroidered with pots and pans. She turned the cauldron round and round in her long, flour-stained fingers.

'Hmm,' she said. 'You seem to have brought the right thing to carry the eternal flame in, so I suppose I'll have to give you some. But there's something I want you to do first.'

Demon's brain immediately went into a panic as he wondered what awful thing Hestia might be going to make him do. The smell of honey cakes was very strong in his nostrils now, and his mouth was beginning to water. He saw that Hestia was holding something small and golden out to him.

'I want you to try this and tell me if it's any good,' she said. 'It's a new recipe for the feast next week. Open up.'

Demon opened his mouth in relief that his task was so easy, and Hestia popped the small golden thing inside. There was a sort of explosion of sweet deliciousness on his tongue. It was the best honey cake he'd ever tasted in his life.

He opened his mouth again. 'More!' he demanded greedily, without thinking that it might be a bit rude to give a goddess orders.

Luckily it was exactly what Hestia wanted to hear.

'Oh goody,' she said, clapping her hands. 'You like them.'

Some time later Demon left Hestia's palace, full to the brim and clutching the cauldron to his chest (plus a box of spare honey cakes). Hestia had given him a lid for the cauldron to keep the eternal flame covered.

'Just promise you won't let Zeus or any of the others see you with that flame,' she said. 'I got into terrible trouble the last time some of it went missing. I'm not supposed to let it out of the palace.'

Demon promised. He tiptoed very carefully past all the palaces, trying hard to be invisible.

Upon returning to the stables Demon tipped the eternal flame carefully down the bull's throat. As he was waiting to see if it had worked, he heard an appalling shriek. It went on and on and on, rising louder and louder and louder until it sounded like all the Furies rolled into one. The Cretan Bull struggled to its feet as its fifth stomach caught light and started to roar like a furnace. But Demon had no time to pat himself on the back. He realised that the shrieking sound was heading straight for the stables.

8

THE PEACOCK CHARIOT

Oh no, thought Demon. *Someone's found out I took the flame out of Hestia's palace.*

He ran up to the loft, hid under his blanket and waited, shivering, to be turned into a little pile of ash. The shrieking stopped. He could hear banging and crashing noises below. Then there was silence.

'STABLE BOY! COME HERE!' said a voice.

It wasn't a nice creamy voice like Hestia's. It sounded like a thousand rusty knife blades snapping in a dark alley. Demon clenched his teeth to stop them from chattering and crawled out from under his blanket. He stiffened his jelly legs and made them climb down the wooden ladder. He could smell the fragrant breath of the unicorns floating up to him like a cloud of sweetness and he wondered if it would be the last thing he ever smelled. Then he reached the ground and fell to his knees, mostly because his legs had turned to jelly again.

In front of him stood six peacocks, their jewelled tails spread out to hide the chariot behind. Demon's heart started to beat its way out of his chest. He didn't even need to see who was in the chariot behind the peacock tails because he already knew. Everyone had told him to keep out of Hera's way, and now here the Queen of the Heavens was in his stables. The peacocks hissed and bent their long necks towards him. Demon scooted backwards hurriedly.

'W-w-what c-c-can I d-d-do for you, Y-y-your G-r-reat G-g-goddessness M-m-majesty,' he asked, just managing to get the words out. He couldn't believe he was still alive. Maybe she hadn't found out he'd taken the flame out of Hestia's palace. Maybe her peacocks were just sick or something.

Hera climbed down from her chariot and walked round the birds to stand in front of him. Demon didn't dare to look up. He stared at her sandals instead. They were made of what looked like golden rats' tails, and they had little onyx and ruby scorpions for buckles. Hera walked round him slowly. Demon felt her eyes pass over him like hot lava. Then she poked him in the ribs with her staff.

'Come with me, stable boy,' she said. 'I've got a job for you.'

Hera strode back to her chariot, and Demon somehow managed to get up and follow her. The peacocks pecked him as he passed them. It hurt but Demon was too glad to be alive to care . . . and at least they hadn't drawn blood. He'd had much worse from the beasts in the stables, anyway.

Hera thumped her staff on the chariot floor. 'Sit,' she commanded.

Demon got into the chariot and sat by her feet, taking care to make himself very small and unobtrusive. Then, quite suddenly, the peacocks wheeled round and started to run. As the birds took flight the chariot swooshed into the air, and the dreadful shrieking started up again. Demon sat on his hands to prevent himself clutching at Hera's robe as they rose higher and higher and then suddenly plunged down with a stomach-sickening lurch, through the misty barrier and towards earth.

Where were they going? Was Hera taking him home to his mum? Demon had about a millisecond's-worth of hope before he remembered. The Queen of the Heavens had a job for him. He had about as much hope of seeing his mum as a worm did in a blackbird's beak. Suddenly the hot, sharp pain of missing Carys hit him right in the guts, as it hadn't for weeks. Demon drew in one quick, sobbing breath, but stuffed the urge to cry into a small corner of his mind. He had a feeling that Hera wouldn't like snot staining the hem of her nice embroidered robes. Quite soon after that, the chariot thumped to a halt and the shrieking stopped again. There was a smell of rotting eggs in the air, and something else . . . something that smelled like blood and fire.

Hera screamed. It was not a scream of fear, but a scream of rage. Demon clapped his hands over his ears, but it was no good. The scream got into every pore of his skin. He felt himself begin to heat up. All the trees around burst into flame and died, leaving small piles of black cinders that blew around in the angry breeze.

'Pleeaasse,' he moaned, feeling the tips of his fingers begin to burn. The scream stopped abruptly and Hera picked him up by the back of his slightly singed tunic.

'Look,' she snarled, shaking him like a rat.

Demon looked as best as he could with his body being whipped back and forth. He sucked his sore fingers. Offy and Yukus were still and silent around his neck, obviously too scared to move.

Lying on the edge of a green and murky-looking swamp was a truly hideous creature. It had nine charred neck stumps, none of which had a head attached. Eight of the obviously chopped-off heads were lying about on the blackened and trampled grass. The ninth head was nowhere to be seen, and the creature looked very dead. Hera flung

Demon down and dropped to her knees.

'Poor little Hydra,' she crooned, patting its thick green hide. 'Did that nasty Heracles cut off your pretty heads, then? Never mind, my sweet, we'll get you all mended again.'

She got up and turned to Demon, who lay wheezing and panting on the ground, trying to get back the breath she'd knocked out of him. Her voice was no longer crooning. The rusty knife blades were back.

'Mend my pet,' she said. 'Prove you deserve your job as stable boy, Pan's son, or I'll send you down to Tartarus as a snack for those revolting hundred-armed monsters quicker than you can say "poo chute".'

Demon had already struggled to his feet and was heading towards the horribly mangled beast. He began picking up heads and loading them carefully into the back of the chariot.

'Is this more of that horrible Heracles' work, Your Goddessness?' he asked, his hatred of the so-called hero making him brave enough to speak.

'Yes,' said Hera. She looked sideways at the

swamp, which began to boil, stinking even worse than it had before.

'Can't you do something about him, Your Goddessness?' asked Demon, who felt angrier than ever with Heracles at the state the poor beast was in.

He began stroking the Hydra's rough skin. It felt limp and cold, but he knew that would change up on Olympus. He remembered Arnie telling him on his first day in the stables that it was only on earth that the immortal beasts could be 'killed'. He hoped that was true, or he was definitely going to be a snack for the hundred-armed monsters.

Hera snarled.

'Insolent stable brat. I'm trying. But Zeus insists that I play by his wretched rules and set the vile man a whole lot of impossible tasks. Otherwise I would have blasted that lowlife hero from the earth already. I can't believe he got past my lovely pet – he must have had help from that scheming Athena. They'll both pay for that.' She pointed her staff at him. The lotus flowers on it spat sparks. 'Now hurry up and stop wasting my time with impertinent questions.'

Demon hurried. He wrapped his silver rope round the Hydra and dragged its mangled body over to the chariot with great difficulty. Then he heaved and lumped it, one leg at a time, on top of its heads. There was still one head missing, though, and Hera was tapping her foot ominously. The ground began to smoke. Demon ran from place to place, searching furiously, but it was no good – the ninth head was nowhere to be seen. He knew he was going to have to risk asking for help. He cleared his throat, which seemed to be full of thistle prickles.

'I'mreallyterriblysorrytobotheryouYourMajestic GoddessnessbutIcan'tfindthelasthead,' he said very fast, before she could turn the staff on him again.

Hera didn't reply. She simply pointed her staff at an enormous rock, black with blood and soot. The rock exploded, and Demon threw himself to the ground as shards and slivers of sharp stone flew past him with a z-z-z-zipping noise like a band of angry hornets. One gashed his cheek open and he could feel the blood dripping down his face.

He looked up cautiously. Where the rock had been was now a hole, and in the hole he could see something glinting. He crawled over to it. There lay the Hydra's ninth head. It had a huge lump of glittering gold set right in the middle of it, just between the eyes. Demon reached into the hole and picked it up. Then he placed it with the other eight heads in the chariot.

Demon thought and thought on the journey back to Olympus, as Offy and Yukus slithered over his cuts and bruises, healing him. How was he going to mend Hera's pet? Hadn't Hephaestus said that getting your head chopped off was fatal? And the Hydra had had all nine of its heads chopped off. That was probably nine times as fatal.

He just hoped the magic medicine box would help him. If it didn't, he was in big, big trouble. Being-eaten-by-hundred-armed-monster trouble, in fact. Demon didn't think he could possibly feel any more scared than he already did. But he reckoned that a trip down the poo chute to Tartarus might just do the trick.

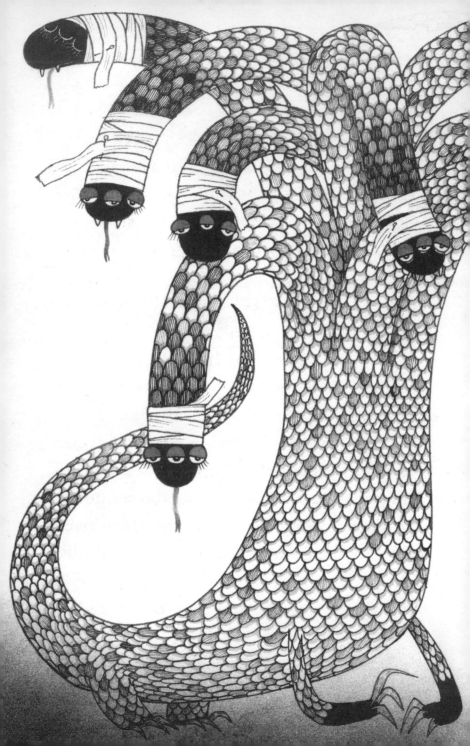

9
THE HYDRA'S FATE

The Hydra rested on the table in the hospital shed, hanging off the edges. It wasn't breathing much. There was just a pathetic-sounding wheeze from one of its throats every few minutes. Its heart didn't seem to be beating at all. All nine heads lay limp and listless. The bandages that attached them to its necks, although neat and tidy, were completely useless.

The magic medicine box had provided him with a huge pot of its usual wound-healing formula and a large paintbrush. Demon had done exactly what it had told him to, but it was no good. Even after he'd fitted the right heads back onto the right necks, the poor beast lay nearly as still and cold as when he had first seen it.

'C'mon, box. Please. There must be something else we can do,' he begged it. But the box remained silent, its numbers now flashing a frantic red instead of the normal blue.

'Error message, error message, error message,' it said over and over again in a high monotonous squawk. It was obviously baffled or broken.

As Demon shut its lid, he began to despair. He thought and thought, but by now he had done so much thinking that his brain just felt tired and full of nothing but fear and worry. Hera had gone back to her palace, but Demon could still hear her last words to him rattling round in his head.

'Remember, stable boy, find out how to mend my pet quickly. Or else.' She had pointed her staff meaningfully in the direction of the muckheaps as the peacocks had started up their infernal shrieking again.

How long did he have before she came back to check on him? Did she even need to check on him? Maybe she had some magic mirror she was watching him in even now. Demon shivered. He badly needed some advice, though, and he needed it at once, since the box was now useless to him. Did he dare leave the Hydra alone to go and see if Hephaestus was back? No. Perhaps he shouldn't risk it, just in case. He stuck his head out of the hospital shed door.

'Althea,' he called. 'Are you there?' There was no reply. 'Althea,' he called louder. Still nothing. 'ALTHEA!' he yelled. Almost at once the nymph floated round the corner of the building.

'All right, all right,' she said. 'Keep your eyebrows on. No need to wake up the whole of Olympus with your shouting. I was busy polishing Aphrodite's camellias for the party tomorrow, if you want to know. Now what is it this time?'

'Could you be a really, really nice nymph?' he asked, smiling his most appealing smile – the one which made his dimples come out and usually worked on his mum. Althea tossed her hair and pouted.

'Depends,' she said. 'Not if it involves offending Hera. I heard those wretched peacocks of hers screeching when they were here. She hates the nymphs enough already, and I don't want to be turned into a cow, like poor Io was.'

'It's only keeping an eye on the Hydra while I go and get Hephaestus,' he said. 'I don't want to leave the poor beast alone while it's in this state. I'll give you a whole box of Hestia's honey cakes if you do,' he added temptingly. Demon knew perfectly well by now that nymphs loved anything sweet. They were always sucking nectar out of the flowers.

'Oh, all right then,' said Althea. 'Hand them over.' Demon ran up to his loft at once. It caused him a pang to see his precious loukoumathes disappearing into Althea's mouth faster than a snake down a drainpipe – but he felt it was well worth losing them if he could help the Hydra and get Hera off his back. 'Yum!' she said indistinctly through a mass of sticky crumbs.

'Send Arnie to Heffy's mountain for me straight away if there's any change at all,' he said. 'I'll be back as soon as I can.'

Once again, Demon was panting as he got to the forge. He dashed in. Hephaestus was back, and Demon felt relief flooding over him. The fire was roaring higher and hotter than he'd ever seen it, and the smith god was banging away with his hammer at a large shield, which was glowing silvery-white in the fierce heat. The noise was indescribably loud.

'Hephaestus! Hephaestus!' shouted Demon, jumping up and down and waving to attract his attention. The automaton robot raised its head and reached out a silvery-gold hand to poke Hephaestus in the ribs. Hephaestus turned his head and saw Demon.

'GET OUT RIGHT NOW!' he bellowed urgently just as the forge flared into the shape of a ferocious-looking dragon head.

Flames billowed out of the dragon's roaring mouth and wreathed the whole forge area in silver-white fire. Demon jumped backwards towards the door just in time. There was a smell of burning hair as his eyebrows and fringe were singed right off. Then there was one last almighty BANG!

from the hammer and the flames died down and retreated with an angry snarl. Hephaestus limped over to Demon, picked him up by the front of his tunic and shook him till his teeth rattled.

'NEVER, NEVER come in when the forge is fired up in dragon mode!' he shouted. 'Didn't you see the notice?'

He flung Demon down in front of a large slab of slate. Carved onto it was a picture of a fearsome dragon spouting fire and a large skull and crossbones. All the fear and worry boiled up inside him and Demon burst into angry tears. He couldn't help it.

'There, there,' said Hephaestus more gently. 'Never mind. But I don't know what I would have said to your dad if you'd been burned to a crisp.'

At the mention of his dad, Demon's tears turned to a hot resentful rage. It was suddenly all too much.

'Why do you think he'd even be worried about me, anyway?' Demon screamed. 'He just dumped me up here and left me. He hasn't been to visit ONCE, even though he promised. I wish I were DEAD. And I soon WILL be. And I don't CARE!'

His nose was dripping snot and he wiped it crossly with his hand.

Hephaestus picked him up, carried him inside the forge and set him down on a table. Then he handed him a length of grimy cloth. 'Stop shouting, blow your nose on this, and tell me what the matter is,' he said, handing Demon a glass of ambrosia.

Demon sipped at it. It tasted as vile as usual, but it did seem to calm him down a bit. He blew his nose loudly.

'It's the Hydra,' he began, sniffing loudly and disgustingly. When he had finished explaining, and told Hephaestus about Hera's threat and how scary and horrid she'd been and about how the magic box wasn't helping, he looked the smith god in the eye. 'I don't think it *can* get better, really. You told me that chopped-off heads were impossible to mend. So I'm doomed to go down the poo chute, aren't I?'

The smith god scratched his head. 'Not necessarily,' he said. 'I think I said *almost* impossible. Let's go and have a look at this Hydra of yours, and then we'll see.'

10

THE MYSTERIOUS TASK

'You do know that Hera's my mother, don't you, Pandemonius?' asked Hephaestus, as he limped slowly towards the stables.

Demon swallowed. He'd forgotten that. And now he'd gone and said how awful and scary she was to Hera's very own son. He opened his mouth to say sorry, but Hephaestus was still talking, so he shut up and listened. He couldn't be in much more trouble than he already was, anyway, he thought.

'I know everyone thinks she's horrible and grumpy – and she is most of the time – but she has got a kind side. Sort of. She made Zeus accept me back on Olympus after he'd thrown me down to earth and smashed my bones up, you know. And she does love her pets in her own grouchy way. I reckon this job of mending the Hydra is some kind of test for you. She could perfectly well cure the beast herself if she wanted to. So you need to use your brains – if there are any inside that thick head of yours.'

He put out a huge hand and ruffled Demon's curly hair. Of course, Demon's brain immediately felt even more like mush than it had before. Thinking was something he'd already done a lot of and he wasn't at all sure he could do any more, let alone the kind that would solve a task set by Hera.

Demon pushed open the door of the hospital shed and went in, Hephaestus following close behind. Althea was floating round the Hydra's heads, humming.

'No change,' she said. 'Now can I *please* get back to polishing Aphrodite's flowers? I've only got about a hundred more to do before supper, and I don't like the smell in here.' With that, she flitted out of the door, flicking a kiss at Hephaestus as she went. 'Don't look so serious, Heffy,' she called over her shoulder. 'It doesn't suit your big old sooty face!'

The Hydra lay exactly where Demon had left it. The magic medicine box lay silent beside it.

'Doesn't look too good, does it?' Demon said. His voice was gloomy and sad – just like he felt, really. Hephaestus hobbled round the beast and poked it with a large grimy finger. The head with the golden lump in the middle wheezed once.

'Not looking too brilliant, I agree. And you say the box couldn't help?' Hephaestus reached over the Hydra's huge green belly and opened the lid. Immediately the box started squawking its error message refrain and flashing red. 'Stupid thing,' said Hephaestus, giving it a thump. 'It's gone and caught one of the viruses it's supposed to cure. Hang on a minute.' He took a large golden screwdriver out of his belt and poked about in the box's innards. It stopped squawking almost immediately.

'State the nature of your beast's medical emergency,' it said in its normal metallic tones.

'Hydra with chopped-off heads that still seems to be nearly dead,' said Demon, hopelessly. It was pretty much exactly what he'd told it before.

The box clicked and whirred, its symbols now returned to their usual clear blue. Demon and Hephaestus waited. And waited. And waited. Finally the box made a clunking sound, and out of it rose a large empty golden bucket and a pot. The pot contained one very large apple seed and some golden-orange earth, which smelled slightly of cinnamon.

'One Hydra cure-all,' it said in its usual smug way. And then it shut down, refusing to say another word.

'What on Olympus do I do with those?' Demon asked Hephaestus. He couldn't for the life of him see how one apple seed, an empty bucket and some soil were going to cure a seemingly lifeless beast with no heads.

Hephaestus began to smile. Then he began to laugh.

'Oh, ho-ho-ho! Very clever. I see exactly what the solution is. That's one very clever box, though I say so myself.'

'Well, I DON'T say so,' said Demon, feeling angry all over again. He hated it when people (or indeed gods) laughed at him. It made him feel all stupid and young, like he was a baby or something. Hephaestus just grinned.

'Oh no – I'm not making it easy for you,' said Hephaestus. 'That would make Hera very upset with me indeed. That box has provided you with everything you need right there, so work it out, boy, work it out. I'll give you just two clues: ask yourself what you cart out of the stables every day, and remember what you know about Hera. Good luck, and hurry up about it – my mother isn't exactly renowned for her patience!'

With that, Hephaestus limped off back towards his mountain.

Demon stamped his foot. Then he looked at the Hydra, lying there all limp and pathetic and wheezy. The most important thing right now was to get it better and to get Hera off his back. He could be properly furious with Hephaestus after that, if he still felt like it. But what about the clues Hephaestus had given him? What was it that he carted out of the stables every day? He paced round and round the Hydra, racking his mushy brain for ideas. Then he smacked himself on the head.

'Of course,' he said out loud. 'Beast poo. That's what I cart out of the stables every day. But what on earth do I do with it? And how does it fit in with the apple seed and the soil and the bucket?' He carried on pacing, trying to remember every fact he knew about Hera, but nothing seemed relevant. Then Arnie poked its beak round the door.

'Everything all right, Pan's scrawny kid?' Demon heard Arnie ask. 'Only everyone's getting a bit smelly and hungry so I let myself out. You haven't been on the evening rounds and we miss your happy little face, not to mention your shovelling skills.'

Demon felt guilty immediately. He'd been so busy trying to find a cure for the Hydra that he'd neglected all the living beasts in the stables. He looked at Arnie.

'Do you think I can leave it on its own?' Demon asked, jerking his thumb at his many-headed patient. He still wondered whether Hera was watching him somehow, but maybe the beasts could give him some clues about her, and that was more important at the moment. At least he would be doing something useful while he thought.

'What? Old Nine Heads? Doesn't look like it's going anywhere anytime soon,' said Arnie. 'C'mon. Hurry up with that ambrosia cake. I'm hungry enough to eat a half-god human.' It snapped playfully at Demon's ear, deliberately missing him by a whisker.

Demon fed all the beasts, then he got his broom and shovel and the barrow and started to muck out. The familiar routine seemed to clear his head.

'Does Hera have anything to do with apples?' he asked Arnie as he swept up bits of glittering silver straw and shovelled them into the barrow.

'Well, Zeus once gave her a tree that produces the golden apples of eternal life,' said Arnie. Demon dropped his broom and stared at the beast.

'What do you mean, eternal?' he asked.

Arnie sighed and looked at him. 'E-t-e-r-n-a-l,' it said, spelling it out very slowly. 'Something that lasts forever. You know the kind of stuff. Immortality and all that. She's got a whole orchard full of them now.'

Demon suddenly felt excited for the first time in what seemed like weeks.

'What exactly do Hera's apples do?' he asked, crossing his fingers and toes for the answer he wanted.

'Well,' said Arnie. 'According to the stories, if you eat a bite of one of Hera's apples, you can be cured of pretty much anything – even being dead.' Its huge eyes widened slightly. 'You're not thinking of going to get one to cure old Nine Heads, are you? Only she keeps her trees at the other end of the world, and they're guarded by Ladon, the dragon who never sleeps, as well as by endless armies of dryads. You'd never make it in a million years – not a little eyebrowless shrimp like you. Even that beastly Heracles had to lie and cheat to get just one, and we all know he's pretty strong and ruthless.'

Demon smiled at Arnie smugly. He knew just

what the apple seed was now, and where it had come from, or he thought he did. He knew what the bucket was for too.

'I don't need to go and get one,' he said. 'I'll just grow my own.'

Arnie gaped at him. It seemed to be speechless for once.

11

THE DRYAD'S MAGIC

Demon had done enough gardening to know that an apple tree didn't normally grow and bear fruit in two minutes flat. However, Hera could come back anytime and his need for a Hydra cure was now more urgent than ever.

But he now had hope.

This was Olympus. Magical things could and did happen here. He filled the golden bucket with beast poo, grabbed the pot of soil and the apple seed and went to find Ophelia the dryad.

Dryads were nymphs who knew all about trees, and he was pretty sure she'd be able to help him. Demon found her at last in the grove near the Iris Express, singing to some blue lemons. He held out the apple seed, the golden bucket of beast poo and the pot of cinnamon-smelling soil.

'Do you know how I can grow an apple from this really quickly?' he asked. 'Only if I don't get one really, really soon, Hera's going to chuck me down the poo chute to Tartarus.'

Ophelia looked at him, her fingers flying up to her mouth. 'Ooh, dear!' she said. 'I heard she visited the stables. What *did* you do to her?'

Demon explained. Then Ophelia took the seed, the bucket and the soil from him. She sniffed at the earth. 'Mmm. Very nice. Did you want a ripe apple, or will a green one do?'

'Ripe, I reckon,' said Demon. 'I don't want to give the poor Hydra a bellyache on top of everything else.'

Ophelia blew on a clear patch of ground at the edge of the orchard and dug a hole with her copper trowel. Then she started to hum a vague little tune. A small cone of dust erupted from the hole and hovered over it. Ophelia poured the bucket of beast poo into the hole first, then added the soil. She mixed them together and finally dropped in the apple seed, which she poked down into the mixture with her finger.

The dust cone collapsed over it, filling the hole to the brim. Then, as her humming got louder, deeper and, somehow, richer, Demon watched in awe as a tiny green shoot erupted from the ground. Within seconds a small tree stood there.

'Wow!' Demon said, leaning forward for a closer look.

Ophelia flapped him away crossly with her free hand. She was using the other one to support the tree trunk. In minutes the tree had grown taller than Demon's head and was covered in golden leaves. One large red bud of blossom appeared on a low branch, then opened into a beautiful flower.

Ophelia started to dance. Round and round and round she went, humming her deep, rich tune (which now seemed to have dark, earthy words twining through it), until Demon felt as if his own feet were growing roots. The red petals floated to the ground and exploded with small pops as an apple began to form where they had bloomed.

It was like no apple Demon had ever seen before. It was perfectly round, like a ball, and it was the colour of a fiery sunset streaked with gold. Demon closed his eyes and sniffed. The apple smelled of everything delicious and wholesome and desirable, and he suddenly wanted to taste it with every part of his being.

'Hey!' said Ophelia. 'Snap out of it!'

Demon opened his eyes and found that the apple was in his hand and touching his lips. She wrenched his hand away. 'If you eat even one bite of that, you'll be immortal. That sounds good, but trust me, Hera will get Zeus to make you pay, over and over and over. Just think about poor old Prometheus chained to that rock with the Caucasian Eagle eating his liver every day. Do you really want to end up with your brains being chewed by a basilisk for eternity – or something even worse?'

Demon dropped his hand to his side with an effort. He was clutching the apple so tightly it should have been bruised, but when he looked down at it, it was as perfect as ever.

'Now,' said Ophelia. 'You'd better get on back to your Hydra, and I'll have a word with this tree. I think it'd be happier as a more normal sort of apple tree, and a lot less dangerous. There's a reason Hera has her orchards at the other end of the world, you know.'

As Demon walked away, Ophelia started to hum again, a different sort of tune this time, and when he glanced back over his shoulder, the tree's leaves were slowly turning to a greeny-bronze. He forced his hand holding the apple to stay away from his mouth, but it was really hard. The smell of the fruit was driving him crazy and by the time he got back to the stables he was drooling with an impossible longing to taste it.

Only the thought of Prometheus, chained to his mountain rock, having his liver torn out for ever and ever, stopped Demon from stuffing the whole apple into his mouth and chomping down. He charged into the hospital shed at a run because he knew that if he didn't get this done, he would give in to the terrible temptation.

He dodged round the Hydra, slammed the apple down on the counter, pulled out a sharp knife from the drawer and cut the apple into nine pieces, a stream of sticky golden juice spurting onto the knife. Demon didn't even notice the tiny droplet falling onto his little finger as he rammed one segment into each of the Hydra's nine mouths, carefully avoiding the rows of sharp pointy teeth.

Almost immediately, twenty-seven marble-like red eyes, each with a round black pupil in the middle, opened and began to roll around frantically. Nine throats breathed in nine wheezy breaths.

'Agghagghah!' said the head with the golden lump, which lay right in the middle of the others. 'Gnoink!' said the other eight. Suddenly, the Hydra's heads all shot upright, its legs began to wave in the air and it heaved itself over and off the table, which fell with a crash against Demon's hand.

'Ouch!' he yelled, stuffing his bruised right

hand into his mouth to soothe the pain. Straight away, he felt a wonderful sensation of warm, succulent coolness travelling over his tongue and down into his body. It was as if heavy golden sunlight had been squeezed over the light of a pure new moon and mixed with concentrated essence of rainbows.

He snatched his hand out of his mouth at once, but it was too late. He'd had the tiniest teeniest taste of the juice of Hera's apple from his little finger. Was he now immortal? It didn't feel like it. But how could he find out unless he did something really stupid, like diving off the stables' roof and seeing if he survived splatting into the ground or not? He felt a twitch around his neck, and put his other hand up to touch Offy and Yukus.

'Am I different?' he asked them in a panicky whisper. 'Am I immortal? Can you tell? Quick! Have a look!'

The two snakes untwined themselves and slithered up and down his body. It tickled, but Demon was too scared to feel anything but panic.

'Perhapsssss you sssseem a ssssmidgen more

magical.' The snaky nostrils sniffed inside his ears. 'Yessss. There issss a ssssmall sssshift.'

'Will Hera notice?' asked Demon urgently. His poor heart was trying to beat its way out of his chest again. There was a pause while the snakes did some more sniffing.

'We ssssussssspect not,' they hissed, as they coiled themselves round his neck again. 'It is infinitesssimally ssssmall.'

Demon wasn't entirely sure what 'infinitesimally' meant, but his heart slowed down a bit. He just hoped Offy and Yukus were right, otherwise there would be worse than the poo chute in store for him.

The Hydra was now nuzzling him inquisitively with two of its heads. Now that its eyes were open, he noticed that it had very long curly eyelashes. Demon had expected it to be like Hera – bad-tempered and dangerous – but he was very relieved that it wasn't. He didn't think that he could have coped with being bitten by nine heads right now – it had been quite a tiring day, all things considered.

'Hey,' he said, stroking it. 'I'm glad you're mended — and not just because I didn't want to go down the poo chute to Tartarus. Now let's go and find a nice big pen for you to live in. Do you feel up to some ambrosia cake?'

The Hydra purred and rubbed up against him again, nearly knocking him off his feet.

Just as Demon was settling the Hydra into its new home, Hera's peacocks shrieked their way into the stables again. The Hydra poked its nine heads over the fence of its pen.

'Muuummmmmmy!' it called. This was the first time Demon had heard it say anything at all. It seemed to be a beast of very few words.

Hera rushed out of her chariot and over to the Hydra, gauzy shawls flying and bracelets rattling.

'Who's my little oochie-coochie pet monster?' she crooned to it.

Demon felt slightly sick. He usually shouted loud insults at anyone who used undignified baby language to animals, but he managed to keep his mouth shut by biting his tongue hard. His mum would have been proud of him, he thought, and anyway, he wasn't risking Hera getting in a bad mood again. He let out a breath he didn't even know he'd been holding. She didn't seem to have noticed his slight shift towards immortality.

'You did well, stable boy,' said Hera. 'The hundred-armed monsters will have to do without their treat this time. In fact, I may even reward you. What would you like best? Jewels?' She gestured with her lotus flower staff and a shower of glittering rubies, sapphires and emeralds fell at his feet. Demon shook his head and tried to stop the Hydra eating them. Hera flicked her staff again and the jewels disappeared. 'No jewels? What then?'

Demon cleared his throat, wiggling his bitten tongue experimentally to see if it still worked. 'I'd like some real food to eat, please, Your Goddessness. If that's all right,' he added hastily.

'Very well,' said Hera. 'I expect I can manage something. I'll talk to Aphrodite. She's in charge of catering this week, so any food you do get is likely to be fluffy and pink and wobbly.' With that, she climbed into her chariot and flew off. Demon just got his fingers into his ears in time to avoid the worst of the peacocks' shrieking.

12

THE FEAST OF
THE GODS

The next morning Demon was cleaning up after
the Cattle of the Sun. He had a new helper in
the stables. The Hydra was following him around
like a large, green nine-headed dog, carrying all
his buckets and brooms and rakes in its nine
mouths. It seemed to be very grateful to him for
saving its life, though it still didn't say very much
other than 'Nice Demon' and 'More ambrosia cake'.

Demon wondered if it had gone a bit simple in the heads after its ordeal. If so, it was one more thing to add to the long list of gripes and grievances he had to thrash out with horrible Heracles when they finally met. Demon's hand tightened on his shovel. He might not like eating ambrosia, but his muscles were definitely getting stronger on this diet. Maybe quite soon he might be in with a chance of getting in a hit or two on that big beast bully before Heracles hit him with that huge ugly club of his . . .

A cherub arrived and cleared its throat crossly at Demon, who was lost in his daydream. Clearly it was not used to being ignored. 'Message from Hera, Queen of Olympus,' it said. 'You are to present yourself at Zeus's palace tonight at the third thunderclap, stable boy.' It fumbled in the pouch at its side. 'Oh, and clean yourself up a bit before you put this on. You can't wear a filthy old rag to a feast with the gods, you know.'

It handed Demon a brand-new white chiton, with a deep band of gold and purple embroidery at the hem and a pair of golden sandals.

Demon was very nervous as the first of the thunderclaps sounded. He walked hurriedly towards Zeus's palace, not wanting to be late. Melanie the naiad had let him use a corner of her spring to wash in, and had even lent him some of the shampoo she used on her own blue locks and then brushed the tangles out of his hair for him. Demon wasn't sure if he liked smelling of watercress and kingcups, but she assured him the goddesses would like it a lot better than his normal smell of straw and poo from the stables.

The white and gold and purple chiton felt softer than anything Demon had ever worn before, and the golden sandals fitted him perfectly, although they felt strange on his usually bare feet. The doors to Zeus's palace were wide open, and there was music and laughter coming from inside.

As the last thunderclap rolled and echoed right above his head, Demon walked in, hoping his stomach wasn't going to rumble. He was hungry enough to eat anything – even pink food if he really had to.

The gods and goddesses of Olympus were waiting for him. Zeus sat on a huge throne in the middle of them all, holding a sizzling lightning bolt sceptre. Demon recognised Hera and Hestia, and there was Hephaestus smiling at him, dressed in white and not sooty for once. Demon dropped to his knees just as he spotted his dad at the end of the table, giving him an encouraging wave. So he'd finally turned up then!

'Pandemonius, son of Pan,' said a booming, thundery voice, which could only belong to the King of the Gods. 'Are you happy in your work?'

Demon dared to look up. 'Yes, Your Great Majesty Godness,' he said. 'It's the best job in the world.' As he said this, he realised it was absolutely true. He'd grown to love his work in the stables, and the beasts who lived there, without really noticing.

'Then approach, Pandemonius.'

Demon got up and walked towards Zeus's throne. For once, he wasn't scared of being turned into a pile of ash. He knelt at Zeus's feet, and the great god placed a wreath of golden laurels on his head.

'I name you Official Beastkeeper to the Gods,' Zeus said, 'with responsibility for all the magical beasts in our realms, and those of our brothers and sisters. You will get seven golden Olympus tokens a month to spend as you wish and you may attend four Olympian feasts a year. Now, let the celebration of our new Beastkeeper begin!'

As he spoke, lightning flashed all round the room, and several little gold and silver trolleys rolled through the doors, smelling of the most delicious things imaginable. Nymphs whisked in with pink-covered tables and couches, and several fauns danced about, playing jewelled flutes.

'Sit by me, son,' said Pan, patting the pink couch beside him. So Demon did, and then Hephaestus came and flopped down on his other side.

'See,' the smith god said, grinning through his beard. 'I knew there was a brain in that curly head of yours. Hera was amazed you worked her little test out, I can tell you.'

'He's not my son for nothing,' said Pan proudly, putting his arm round Demon. 'Definitely a sapling off the old tree, eh, Heffy?' Demon just felt annoyed at his dad's attention. It was all very well him trying to take credit for Demon's success, but where had he been when Demon needed him? Pan squeezed him tighter, and cleared his throat.

'I'm sorry I haven't been up here to see how you were getting on, old chap,' he said. 'Time seems to have got away from me a bit. It passes differently up here. Those satyrs of mine, you know. They take a lot of handling.' He coughed in an uncomfortable way, as Hephaestus rolled his eyes.

'Your boy has done you great credit, Pan,' said the smith god. 'I don't know how those beasts ever managed without him.' Demon turned as red as a raspberry. All this praise was making him feel a bit wriggly. Delicious smells were wafting past his nose now, and he was ravenous.

Luckily the food arrived just then. What food it was! Dishes of roasted pigeons with yoghurt and almonds, garlicky roasted lamb's legs with crispy rosemary, chicken and lemon soup, sweet figs and tart, creamy cheese, Hestia's delicious honey cakes, apricot tarts, fresh peaches and strawberries and exotic fruits and nuts from the ends of the earth. Some of the carts held food that was pink and wobbly and fluffy, as Hera had predicted, but there was so much else on offer that it was easily avoided. Demon ate and ate and ate till his tummy was like a tight little drum. Tomorrow he might have to go back to horrible old ambrosia again, but tonight . . . tonight he would feast on Olympus as the one and only Official Beastkeeper to the Gods.

GLOSSARY

BEASTS:

Basilisk (*BASS-uh-lisk*): King of the serpents. Every bit of him is pointy, poisonous, or perilous.

Chiron (*KY-ron*): A super-centaur – part horse, part man, with all the best parts of each.

Cretan Bull (*KREE-tun*): A furious, fire-breathing bull. Don't stand too close.

Griffin (*GRIH-fin*): Couldn't decide if it was better to be a lion or an eagle, so decided to be both.

Hydra (*HY-druh*): Nine-headed water monster. Hera somehow finds this loveable.

Ladon (*LAY-dun*): A many-headed dragon that never sleeps (maybe the heads take turns?).

Minotaur (*MIN-uh-tor*): A monster-man with the head of a bull. Likes eating people.

Nemean Lion (*NEE-mee-un*): A giant, indestructible lion. Swords and arrows bounce off his fur.

Stymphalian Birds (*stim-FAY-lee-un*): Man-eating birds with metal feathers, metal beaks and toxic dung.

THE GODS AND GODDESSES:

Aphrodite (*AF-ruh-DY-tee*): Goddess of Love and Beauty and all things pink and fluffy.

Ares (*AIR-eez*): God of War. Loves any excuse to pick a fight.

Athena (*a-THEE-na*): Goddess of Wisdom and defender of pesky, troublesome heroes.

Artemis (*AR-te-miss*): Goddess of the Hunt. Can't decide if she wants to protect animals or kill them.

Dionysus (*DY-uh-NY-suss*): God of Wine. Turns even sensible gods into silly goons.

Hades (*HAY-deez*): Zeus's youngest brother and the

gloomy Ruler of the Underworld.

Helios (*HEE-lee-us*): The bright, shiny and blinding God of the Sun.

Hephaestus (*Hih-FESS-tuss*): God of Blacksmithing, Metal, Fire, Volcanoes and everything awesome.

Hera (*HEER-a*): Zeus's scary wife. Drives a chariot pulled by screechy peacocks.

Hestia (*HESS-tee-ah*): Goddess of the Hearth and Home. Bakes the most heavenly treats.

Poseidon (*puh-SY-dun*): God of the Sea and controller of supernatural events.

Zeus (*ZOOSS*): King of the Gods. Fond of smiting people with lightning bolts.

OTHER MYTHICAL BEINGS:

Cherubs (*CHAIR-ubs*): Small flying babies. Mostly cute.

Dryads (*DRY-ads*): Tree spirits. Only slightly more serious than nymphs.

Epimetheus (*ep-ee-MEE-thee-us*): Prometheus's silly brother who designed animals. Thank him for giving us the platypus and naked mole rat.

Geryon (*JAYR-ee-un*): A cattle-loving giant with a two-headed dog.

Heracles (*HAIR-a-kleez*): The half-god 'hero' who just loooves killing magical beasts.

Naiads (*NYE-ads*): Water spirits: Keeping Olympus clean and refreshed since 5,000 BC.

Nymphs (*NIMFS*): Giggly, girly, dancing nature spirits.

Pandora (*pan-DOR-ah*): The first human woman. Accidentally opened a jar full of evil.

Prometheus (*pruh-MEE-thee-us*): Gave fire to mankind, and was sentenced to eternal torture by bird-pecking.

Satyrs (*SAY-ters*): 50% goat, 50% human. 100% party animal.

Silenus (*sy-LEE-nus*): Dionysus's best friend. Old and wise, but not that good at beast-care.

PLACES:

Arcadia (*ar-CAY-dee-a*): Wooded hills in Greece where the nymphs and dryads like to play.

Tartarus (*TAR-ta-russ*): A delightful torture dungeon miles below the Underworld.

Don't miss Demon's next exciting adventure . . .
in the Underworld!

OUT NOW